Carnival of Longing

Carnival of Longing

Kristjana Gunnars

Turnstone Press

Turnstone Press
607-100 Arthur Street
Winnipeg, Manitoba
Canada   R3B 1H3

Turnstone Press gratefully acknowledges the
assistance of the Manitoba Arts Council and the
Canada Council.

Cover illustration by Gudmundur Thorsteinsson,
from the book *Sagan af Dimmalimm*, published by
Helgafell, Reykjavík. Thorsteinsson, commonly
known as "Muggur," was a poet, singer and
painter born in Iceland in 1891 who died at the
age of 30.

Cover design: Kelly Fraser Design

This book was printed by Hignell Printing
Limited for Turnstone Press.

Printed and bound in Canada.

Canadian Cataloguing in Publication Data

Gunnars, Kristjana, 1948-

  Carnival of longing

  Poems.
  ISBN: 0-88801-139-3

I. Title.
PS8563.U663C3 1989   C811'.54   C89-098107-8
PR9199.3.G866C3 1989

Acknowledgements

The cycle "Dimmalimm" received second prize in the CBC literary competition for 1986 and was aired on CBC's "State of the Arts."

The cycle "Cheekeye" was a finalist in the CBC literary competition for 1987.

Parts of the cycle "Sunlamp" appeared in *Canadian Woman Studies'* special issue on Nordic women in 1988.

for Béla

Contents

I.
Dimmalimm

you have made me tire of words
the universe, the birds, the customs
of people as they fidget through the days

in the heat I am fatigued
after rain, thunder, the muggy air
weighs the body down. the small black
flies that flurry up from the grass
where you put your foot. you are walking

my head full of words that will
not be written, cannot be written
my body filled with the sorrow
the heat of the day

that comes of this separation
the loss, the siamese twins
surgically removed. I long for your
walking step through the grass
and cannot speak

this longing silenced: as black-
mail, as pressure, as love
that must not be voiced
this scar I must not show

the words that are gathered in my body

the great hydroelectric plant that is my language

the dam that contains them, the spirit

you have cracked, there are leaks

my father who loved me, I could tell, that which was never spoken. a certain red sweater my mother knitted and I wore, the same every day, and black rubber boots. in my father's jeep we went, I did not know where, into the mountains, obscure gravel roads, to the great dam. in those boots I hung over the railing above the stilled pooling water while my father spoke with the men. always speaking with the men.

it is not me who weeps
it is my body
a thing apart

if I said I was weeping I would say
it is Romantic, belongs
to another age
if I told you I wept unaccountably

because you are not here
there is longing, a sense of loss

and no image for this body weeping
that longs for you
from another age

unaccountably embarrassed by itself
it cannot be me

my mother and father, in the kitchen, their voices raised, arguing. I walked down the hall, back and forth, uncertain, my mother's voice demonstrative, with pain, my father's also. wanting to go in and not wanting to go in, their voices were the hard edges of my childish sorrow. they made me weep and I could not explain the weeping, they made me embarrassed. then always, in the end, I opened the door, something like a beggar in the doorway, asking them not to argue. the beginning of a beggar's life.

I have heard speakers on silence
an aesthetics of the negative
the value of a pause
an ellipsis of voice

but silence as it is when you live it
destroys the aesthetic
there is nothing poetic about silence

it is an absence without image
poem without content
without metaphor
poem of mere words

silence/absence
what cannot be said without you

the night lingers: a slow lover
refusing to leave
clinging before dawn

the night is my uninvited terror
loving me

I hear scuffles in the grass outside
the moon blazes: a voyeur
staring in through the window

where I have allowed myself to lie naked
in a triumph of reason
the moon is only moon

in the July heat
meshed in the croaking of the crickets
the humid night lies on me

a misty body
laughing at me, triumphantly
to say he is not you

in my room I had knitting needles and wool. in the evenings I knitted, the door closed. on my wall were pictures of Dimmalimm, watercolours, about a princess alone by a pond, looking into the water. and a swan. Dimmalimm was sad and cried a great deal in every picture. it was a mystery to me why she should be alone and why the forest behind her was so soggy, so dreary, so unpeopled. they said the painter Muggur was melodramatic. he was in love. he was in my family. I knitted and thought about kinship.

the words I write attempt
no meaning and use
no image

it is a non-writing
a series without last words
what cannot be said of desire
with desire

that I try to keep the persistent
influx of you
out of my thoughts

your voice, your hair, your eyes
images dark, black, the smile
always half faint on your lips

that I have no memory of your hands
your imperceptible body
deprived of the last traces of you

no memory of your promises
I write without memory

our future love is without being
it is desire
a point of sorrow
where I am lost

it is a love of the banal
the insignificant
that which is not powerful

the love of small matters
the way you walk in the dark
not to wake me

the way you nod when you have understood
how you plan ahead
how you forget things everywhere

life itself is insignificant
not effective
a series of days and nights

thoughts of you make me happy
whether or not I am with you

it is a love of the final statements
that allow us to sleep

I wake in my private study
knowing how ridiculous
feelings are

and construct a carnival of my longing
laugh at myself in the amphitheatre
with clowns and roller coasters

my mother scolded me. whatever I did was wrong. I lied, I stole coins from her pockets, coats hanging in the hall. I was always late coming home at night, late to leave in the mornings, too slow to pack my suitcase, dawdling over insignificant details. I was late for school. time never lined up right. I was not what I was supposed to be. finally I packed some dried fish in a knapsack and left home, walked off, humiliated by myself.

Muggur was the first to go abroad and leave a trail of broken hearts behind him. he died young. he could paint, act, sing. he wrote Dimmalimm. in Norway he was arrested by a woman in love and imprisoned in the mountains. in Denmark he acted in movies. he was Scandinavia's wonder, darkly handsome, his hair falling into his eyes and a mischievous smile. I read this in the paper, he was my granduncle and a painting of his hung in the living room.

the past is a fiction
history is a beloved story

it is an onion
peeling off in layers, without centre

is an orange, wedges falling
a bowl of rice, etc.

in the story of you and me
likewise fiction, improbable

segments fall off at a touch
I find myself in pieces

true crime, etc.
a detective novel

I do not want to write
what there is to write
words are ironic
they speak of themselves
and say what I had not intended

that my body is an illness
is a guilty animal
seeking cure, absolution
studying the orthodox

in the night a train whistles through
and trucks pass on the perimeter
a steady humming that says
we the wakeful

I do not want the words
to give absolution, communion
unordained blessings
words are powerless for that
poetry is a marginal note

does not answer questions
does not bring lovers back
poetry is a humiliated child
leaving home in the night

and it will never speak of us
as we are
in signs of a dead language
orthodox sinners
unconnected sayings

the morning heat deprives me
even of thought, that comfort
always entertaining

the empty square outside
the gathering clouds
the promise of rain
air drenched in water, heavy

even in this deprivation
your presence persists
without image
there is no picture of you

only that you which is
my body, that drenched
feeling of your intrusion

and this muggy air is without thought
forgetful of detail
desirous of immersion

without the elegance of a good poem

all my words may speak another story
depending on the reading
a Freudian story, Jungian
Lacanian, Barthesian, auto-
biographical story
when I had not intended to tell
any story

only to voice an unhappy
utterance of no import
using matte language, without
reverberation, a flat language
of concern to no one
that I desire you

the absent one, and am
therefore inundated with words
I am the air charged
with electricity, that weight
before a thunderstorm
a Prairie deluge

that I am calm
in spite of myself
telling stories incompetently
without my own permission

I cannot remember happy moments in my childhood. those years were full of menace, unspoken terrors, a vision in the night of a point, a distant point that comes nearer and presses me, contracts me inside it until I am condensed within a single point. it was a radioactive feeling of invisible weight and I was unable to express it, explain it. I would go out of my room and into bed between my parents where the point would not venture. they lay on each side of me, putting up with me for a time, what they called my silly hysteria.

I went about as a child seeking love. I found parents in my parents' friends, I found relatives in the neighbours. I had my own room in many houses, I was taken in. I loved deeply, these people who took me in, a silly girl whom they indulged. I lived in the red house at the bottom of the fjord. I lived in a new house in the north end. I lived in the basement with the old couple. I was a beggar for love. searching for a self I could take with me when I went away, someone who was not silly.

there is pleasure in describing
the birdcall in the distance
the way its song echoes
in the empty air

pleasure in speaking of the grass
wet with dew
unevenly green and lazy
the bushes tired, fatigued

the white butterfly across my path
cruising the way I cruise
between distractions
until distraction is central

pleasure in allowing
the unimportant to take hold
not to be useful
not to be sensible

the sense that to be in love
is to be distracted
to desire is to be waylaid
to be a mad fool

suddenly writing about butterflies

we were Scandinavian Lutherans. it was something grim that did not allow pleasure except with guilt. the pleasure of wasting time or of being useless, the pleasure of play. as a child I had chores; to wash, dust, iron, care for small children, look after them in play-yards. my mother did not want to find me being useless. to daydream was forbidden. my daydreams became my secret sin, the forbidden act, the stolen pleasure. I was a thief, a fool, an incestuous wrong-doer: I daydreamed all day long, while working, and no one knew.

II.
Gullfoss

no snow falls
no sun shines
a day of nothing
winter without winter

you are not here
nothing I can say
will make words of nothing

my desire to speak is as strong
as my desire to be silent
water ebbing and turning
in childhood pools

memory deserts me
there is no knowledge in this thought
except the empty sense
I desert myself

the sense of your absence
that words cannot fill
without flesh, without touch
these words are pebbles

tossed into a tidal pool
of what I have done
what I have written that is wrong

the night refuses to be cold
deprives me of preparations
steals in on the afternoon
too gentle to be noticed

time passes without my knowing
I watch the numbers on the clock
slip by without effort

time is where you are
your silent steps down the stairs
your silent breath when you sleep
your imperceptible touch

when you are not you
but I in another form
a shadow of what is forgotten
when your face is my face

looking back at me
trying to say with your eyes
what that time was like

when I really was you
and you were the air I breathed
dark and indistinct
you were the night in me

in winter there are no colours
no gossamer webs
in the grass in the dew

only barren branches above the fence
and crusty brown leaves that refuse to let go

only the silence of spreading frost

when I was very young I collected guilt instead of coins or stamps or serviettes. I stole scarves from a warehouse, bills from a cash register. I climbed out of my bedroom window at night. I hid among the rocks while the police searched for me, afraid to go home, afraid to stay. my mother tried to lecture me while I crouched in the corner. my father took me aside and closed the door, then sat in exasperated silence, unable to speak.

I have written words to you
and I imagine they have become knives
that my words injure

you find them on your floor in the mornings
you stumble over them in your bedroom
at night when the lights are out

and they are cutting you
they are turning into pain

I write more words to soothe the scars
to take the former words back
and the new words are knives

and there is never an end
love mars, love betrays me
a language that steals away from me

and grows in shadows around you
the mooning doves at your window
whisper nightmares as you sleep

I imagine I have marred
the perfect beauty that was you
this love that has clung
like stubborn winter leaves

has worn you down
the way water wears down stone
by constant thought
constant desire

that the hands that love you
your limbs, muscles, hair
are the slow disease of acid rain

I watch you age
the time I have longed for you
under the continuous needles
of poems that are of no use

words that have made this statue move
that have softened the perfect joints
and made this stone face weep

your face
the first face I ever saw

from the earliest days it was first in my mind to undo what I had done. I dried my mother's dishes, scrubbed her floor, dusted her shelves and cabinets. I ironed her clothes, meticulously attempting to straighten every crease. I waited with her at the bus stop, her tall figure facing the wind from the sea. she went into the bus and the door closed. I was left leaning against the bus stop sign, watching her drive away, her back to me, and what I did was never enough.

the mild winter morning
when birds have ventured out to sound
against the grey sky
knowing their tiny voices
will not hurry the sun

knowing my poem will not move
snow to melt or grass to sprout
nonetheless I write

incompetent against the great clouds
my poem a form of breathing
a form of longing
to say over the frozen snow

that I think of you
without thought
that your image like a dream
recedes when sought
that the memory of spring is old
and of another world

the only country I knew to be mine was a ship that sailed the Atlantic. it was Gullfoss that took us from Copenhagen to Glasgow and Reykjavik so often I forgot I lived anywhere else. floating in the womb of the hull I forgot the sensation of solid ground. alone in my bunk under a porthole, the cabin creaking and curtain swaying, it was where I felt at home. when Gullfoss was in harbour my knees would bend by themselves, attuned to the uncertainty of the sea.

the ship Gullfoss was my mother. it was my home. the wooden banisters, the steep stairs, the tilting floor described the interior of a world I knew. the possibility of whales and sharks below my feet. the black tar of ocean, the sunset on the sea. the loneliness of tracing our course on the green map on the wall. Gullfoss was sold to a Greek shipping company. I read this in the paper. it sank to the bottom of the Aegean, my home a futile dream.

I do not want my words to grow
and become important monsters
I no longer recognize

I want my stories to be small
castaway bottles
their contents drained

no story can describe
what it is to love uncertainly
there are no words for those shadows

how you stare at the sun
how you take my hand in your sleep
averting some private terror

what it is to stand on the deck
knowing forms are swimming below
the surface of sleep

that holding your hand will not keep you
from sinking or drifting away
and by some error of the imagination

I have made words of a dream
that is nothing but longing
nothing but desire

I said my taskmaster was death

the one who passes behind you through the doorway

the one who reclines beside you in the chair

the one who rises before you in the morning

and places his arm around you
loving you away from me

sunlight steals onto the snow
and two clinging cats
follow me down the road

you are breaking the snow
the freezing wind in your face

I imagine you walking
but what I see in the city park
is another image of me

as indistinct as I am to myself
the one I cannot face
the one I cannot walk beside

I do not remember my mother who sailed us back and forth. we had no school on board, no athletic competitions, no ballet classes. only the sea and empty Pilsner bottles I stole from the bar. in the ship's lounge there were leather chairs and playing cards. like Ingrid Bergman my mother sat in the lounge with the captain, surrounded by coffee and smoke. I wrote my address on paper for someone to find and stuffed it in a bottle. between the Faroe Islands and Iceland I threw the bottle overboard.

III.

you are forcing me to be myself
my own wind, my own aspen leaves
in the morning, my own sun

the shadow of ants
the white clouds scattered
and parched grass, yellowing

and I do not want myself
in the doorway, at the window
on the back steps, I reject

that force that was to have been
me, that world
I would otherwise have made

there is no world without you

I know the banality of such
statements, the commonality
of such sentiments of desire

my love for you embarrasses me

I am walking in my own shadow

I am pretending to be myself

I put up a front: in the bookstore
the art gallery, the café
at my own table

I claim to be where I am

and I am not
I am not where you are either
I am not remembered

all I am is my love for you
humiliated

I have heard of the end of writing

an animal that attacks the fleas
in its fur, bites irritably
lies down on the steps, watching

when all texts soak into the grass:
yesterday's rain, glistening
fine drops in the afternoon

it is an end we have waited for
words known to be mere words
a cessation of power

I have found this end
where the ink I spend is useless
the page fills for no reason

an animal with closed eyes
voicing itself in empty space
where hearing has ceased

and it amazes me
how life continues
how passions do not subside

how at this end I am still
writing, writing you
through my bones

I do not remember being myself

I think I have expected you all my life

IV.
Sunlamp

we were afraid of leprosy because it was epidemic once in the north. but that was not it the doctor said when I showed him my blotched skin. I was maybe nine and found my body one morning covered in an unknown rash. it is nothing the sun will not cure he said, and salt water. I waited for sunshine so I could expose my skin and be healed. but the clouds did not break and there never was any sun. a condition of waiting for what never showed.

my parents, attempting to take over the work of God, bought a sunlamp so it could shine on me. so began the hours of darkness that filled my childhood. it was a strict routine I was honour bound to follow in order to be normal again. every day the door was closed and I was left in a dark room, naked before the glow of the lamp. it was an ominous metallic light that made the room smell like the burning of limestone and I knew it was dangerous. I knew it was somehow a replica of life to react to danger by taking the clothes off and lying down beside it.

I was trying to think with those dark glasses that covered my eyes to shield them from the unnatural rays. but the thoughts would not appear. instead I took note of the atoms that floated in the air between me and the lamp, small points of hard metal that struck my skin. and from this the clear sensation that they were invading my body to lodge there for life, to harden me inside.

I vowed my friends would never know about that other life, the one I lived in a dark room. when they asked me to the handball court or the track field or to climb in unfinished buildings I said simply I had something to do. I was fulfilling a sinister contract with an electric object that masqueraded as the sun. the object smiled at me a broad neon smile that stuck on its face for as long as I stood bony and naked before it.

what I thought of as my hours of darkness were only minutes. ten minutes, fifteen minutes, twenty minutes, adjusting my unprotected skin to the rays. it was a light by which I could not see and it shone without illumination. I was ordered to keep my eyes closed or I would go blind. it was not possible to read or think or tell the time that passed as heavily as if it were made of iron. no one dared to come near the lamp that had become my unwanted companion. not even my mother, who only knocked on the door and called to me it was time to turn the other side.

you have made me think of my childhood
the silent years
of waiting, of pressing
unlikely sorrows inside me
and longings of disbelief
that I will wake up suddenly to find
it was only a dream, all
only a dream

you are my parents, you are
the ship we sailed, the distant
relative who wrote fairy tales
and watercoloured images of the other
me locked in the dream
or locked in the reality of which
I was the dream

this early life that so resembles
an Ingmar Bergman film
where we go about thinking thoughts
never expressed, where no one says
what he means, where everyone knows
this is a film we are in
an unhappy film due to end

and I long to arrive at that end
to stop seeing the reel of images
pass by in still succession, I long
to rise from this wooden bench
with you and walk out of the dark
room holding your arm

I have discovered there are no degrees of love
no levels that go higher
or lower, no altitudes of thinning air

it has no measure, it cannot be
surveyed, counted, marked
with signs, numbers, arrows

love is not a mountain we climb
or a cavern into which we descend
it is not a hall of mirrors or a carousel

or an ocean infested with sharks
or a story that begins and ends
and it is not bound or covered

and yet love is
an existence apart, I have discovered
it is my life

an existence gone through because of you
without comprehension, without knowledge
all things leading up to you

and after all, it is all I have
to offer, I sometimes think
this love is all I am

and what I thought of as undetected leprosy went away, leaving trace ruins of where it went over me like high tide over the stones in the shore. it was the sun-lamp they said and if you are in the dark too long without it, if you live under clouds, it will all come back. I took care to bathe in the sun the few times it shone. I lay in the garden behind the house, in the grass mounds by the water in the fjord, or wherever I could not be seen and my defect discovered.

there is also terror in my thoughts of you

that there is something I will be
unable to hide from your
intense eyes, that I will blunder
make a mistake, that you will notice
the other me

that there is another me in the shadows

a certain terror that as you love me
after you have given yourself
your mouth, skin, arms, everything
that is you has been offered

and we have been in the dark too long
you will turn on the light and find
I have changed. and again I will be
speechless, unable to explain

it was dark for too long and I wanted
you too much, I could not
help it, and instead
you will see that smaller person
who has been hiding in me so long

defective, crouching behind her knees
covering her face and eyes
from the glare of the dangerous rays

the late evening sun flows sideways
onto the Trappist monastery of St. Norbert
accentuates the deep greens and golds
of sun bleached limestone and dark
pines before the pale fields

the monastery stands in its ruins
broken walls half hoping to the sky
wind swept openings where windows had been
gutted by fire. small birds
now sing the litanies of open echoes

we have been wandering here, my son and I
that boy who has grown beyond recognition
not fully knowing this was at our back door
a vacated grandeur, a sudden beauty
of walls accidentally exposed

the hopes of tranquillity, solitude
desire for peace, ravaged by chance
calamity flooding like high tide
over the stones on the shore
leaving bony ruins and true silence

into which the Manitoba sun pours
and that boy has been climbing the walls
without memory, without thought
admiring the half leprous limestone
and I am glad he is made so free

I do not understand time
the sudden passing and abrupt jumps
from one time to another
large gaps lost, outside memory

I do not know where our life has gone
whether we have gone through it
bravely or not, mistakenly or not
and there is much I do not remember

large days without you
when you have receded out of focus
perhaps in the whistle of the train
burrowing by at night

waking me from sleep
the speeding alarm on its rails
that says there is something we forgot
and the walls are shaking

this is not a gentle summer

the grasses quiver with discomfort
the sparrows race from roof to roof
in some search of the missing
the noise of electric saws and lawnmowers
can be heard grinding things down

even the white butterfly shows despair
endlessly searching among the clovers
and the breeze in the aspen leaves above me
intimates there is no rest

I am propelled by my sense of loss

the morning sun does not succeed
in comforting me, the fresh smell
of prairie grasses refuses to reach me

I have lost you even in your affirmation
that I cannot lose you

I cannot account for this emptiness

the train passes at noon with bells and whistles

children scatter off the railroad tracks

the sound of rumbling engines burrows over us

grinding down with its heavy force and strewing

that part of me that is you

in spite of what those we called adults said, my private conviction told me the sunlamp was not effective. it was a grinning impostor, glaring at the world. when the condition of my skin persisted and crept to my face I could no longer pretend it was not there. I steeled myself with thoughts of bravery and went about my business, to school, to the milk shop, on my paper route. wherever I needed to go. I do not remember anyone in the world reacting. I discovered it was a defect to which everyone but me was blind.

I thought I had made a pact with death

that in return for my sorrow
he will spare those I love most

so I have claimed you
I tell myself he cannot take you
because you are mine

V.
Cheekeye

I do not think the leaves are falling
although they lie on the grass
mustard and brown in bunches
along the path where we walk

leaves do not fall in this world
they blow forward with the wind
and rustle in groups up the street

this is an autumn I cannot contain
in the language on which we are carried
what we wanted to say but know
that is not what we meant to say
before we say it

so we are silent, hoping perhaps
the breath that is ourselves is passed
in a brief touching of hands
or a look as we close the door

thinking there are very few trees
in spite of the many leaves

I have often said
that what I have said cannot be said
that every verbal construct is just
words on paper
and does not concern you

we call them empty words
and think we can laugh at our games
since nothing needs to be said

yet I think it needs to be said
so the life I live will not be
the child that never was
an impossible possibility

the memory of snowflakes
the anticipation of frost
simple things like the torture
of what is left untouched
or the unwritten poem

the one that continues from a former
unwritten poem and ends
in anticipation instead of ending

if poems are written in knowledge
there are no poems in me
what I know is only tentative
my arms, hands, mouth
hold only the air that blows
in rust coloured autumn winds

all I know is you
the way you rush my words away
before they are spoken
before I knew what I was going to say
you have taken my speech

this paltry search for meaning
the cats that meander down your alley
the bicycle thief who falls down on the gravel
the native who sleeps on the pastor's grass
in the afternoon when I walk by

and if it is love to give your speech to another
then it is love I feel
when I do not reply
but listen to you say these things
knowing the sun is descending

and you want me there when you die
and when I die only you
will be on my lips
and how is it I have become you

when I knew I knew nothing and had no pretensions it was simpler. our cabin on the Cheekeye Indian reserve had two rooms and from both I could hear the continuous rustling of the Cheekeye River. it was not pastoral or idyllic. it was just there. a cabin and a river and mountains where the Cheekeye kids searched for bears and came to tell me what they saw. I was alone during the day and now and then a dark haired girl appeared at my front door thinking I spoke more than one language.

is it an Indian boy you married? the Dutch miner on sick leave with an infected hand said. I was serving the coffee he purchased in a Squamish café. the one I see working on the railroad at the warehouse he said and I wanted to lie. I said yes. I would have said it does not matter whom I have married or what he does or what he is. but that is not it at all.

perhaps they had no interest or they were afraid of approaching. but the women asked what do you do up there? in the cabin all day behind closed doors. I read books I said. I have been to the Hudson's Bay store and bought a bag full of books. and when I do not read the books I collect pebbles on the Cheekeye riverbank. whatever I do it has no purpose and I know it has no purpose. I brought the pebbles into the cabin with me thinking perhaps the river would follow.

I think you do not hear what I say
that in my silence you are deaf

all those words, letters, phone calls
even the words in your arms
and the ones lying beside you in the bed
the whispered, hesitant words

have fallen in crumbs on the floor
I see them when I arise
careful not to wake you

barefoot on the floor I feel them
attach themselves to my feet
clinging to me, frightened children

following me into the kitchen
pressed between me and the floor
telling me things I never said

that nothing we say can move us

that in love words are like the birds
that smash themselves onto the window
and fall down dazed on the ground

that when I speak it is just
the sound of a distant train
that long since passed our hearing

yet I collect your words

what you say is gathered in pebbles
deposited along the riverbank

thinking perhaps someday I will remember
how they came down from the mountain

groups of dark haired children
running from grizzly bears

telling me incoherently of fears
and narrow escapes on the edges of cliffs

they were in the beer parlour. the parents. brothers. sisters. grandma and grandpa. uncles. a large family group around a table. smiling that I was among them having a beer because if you do not go to a beer parlour here they will ask you what you do all day alone in the cabin. there was a pool table and I played pool until the heavy hand of a Squamish pulp mill worker took me by the collar. you get out of here if you know what's good for you he said. I cannot say I was thrown out of my own country. that is not what I said.

I think the wind is between us

I know the wind gushes
over miles of cold prairie
where nothing else is
but ground and sky

all that emptiness between us
that reminds me of what passes
lives we have lived

in the light of my only lamp
the past vanishes like darkness
and I can see in this present
you are not here

you are not within hearing
and the windows rattle in the storm

I do not need to renounce the knowledge
I do not have
there is nothing I can give up
that was ever mine

and if I have made you my life
it is because you have always been

I do not want to make statements
declarations that will freeze us
as winter settles

not about love
because I do not know where limits are
or how far feelings go
and not about misgivings
that are always present

these are the limits of winter itself
the migrating geese going south
the pigeons cooing at your window all year

a penniless Cree couple
peddling their children's toys on the street
a bone thin hooker in stilt heels
bruised in her swollen face

scenes of a world that is not pretty
passing us by like an unhappy film
and now when I come down in the morning
I can feel the cold draft from the door

I am glad you offered me your life
before I could confess my terror
you would not have understood

I think you would not understand
what life without you is like

it is not the name of the Cheekeye girl I remember but her long black hair and slight smile. when the Norwegian oil tanker docked in Squamish and the girls went on board. there was hope in that look when she appeared at my cabin and told me her life. she would go to the city she said and learn hairdressing but behind her story there was another thought. about the Norwegian sailors. she thought she had discovered the other language. that other language I knew.

that unsophisticated and powerless person that was me still lodges in my consciousness. the one who loved the smell of the wood in the cabin. who watched the train head by into the deep mountains. who stood on the bridge above Cheekeye River watching water flow. there was nowhere to go then. no one to meet. no deadlines or schedules. just the sunrise squeezing its thin rays through the massive fir trees at my door. only my education tells me it was a wasted life. that knowledge I never wanted.

you have made me want to go back
and put away the pretense
that has layered itself on my bones
like rings on a tree

as if there really were a backwards and forwards
to the lives we lead
as if time had a direction
a tightrope we could walk at will

you have made me think I am performing
attempting amazing feats in a circus
a balancing act without a net
with lights and music

and if love dispels all illusions
then it is love I am holding
as the carnival noise dims
and the glaring lights go out

in spite of that postcard nature I cannot say it was a happy time. when grandma and grandpa came to the Squamish café for Sunday steak and then fell asleep in their booth. when old Henry stood and yelled at those around him they had forgotten their native tongue. when that young Robert whose wife had just run away to Prince Albert played Tom Jones on the jukebox over and over. in order not to be alone in his turquoise house with the totem pole and automatic dryer in the front yard.

you have made me face that face
that has been hiding behind my back
the one that knows
there is a terror to confess

about being trapped in an unhappiness
a deep sea from which
I never emerge
a misfortune of origin

that is also a revelation
about living in a hall of warped mirrors
and there really is nowhere to go

I do not want to write words
about ultimate ends
but you told me to be careful
so you will not lose me
you said you will take care of me

and I am grateful for your words
I hold them against my chest
white rounded pebbles
deposited by the hurrying river

and although such stones do not break down
I cannot say they contain much comfort
for you yourself who spoke them
are only an outline of my hopes

a shadow of my incomplete memory
an uncertain knowledge
that if you are not
this can no longer be me